To all critters

SIMON & SCHUSTER BOOKS FOR YOUNG READERS
An imprint of Simon & Schuster Children's Publishing Division
1230 Avenue of the Americas, New York, New York 10020
© 2023 by Amy June Bates
Book design by Laurent Linn © 2023 by Simon & Schuster, Inc.
SIMON & SCHUSTER BOOKS FOR YOUNG READERS and related marks are trademarks of Simon & Schuster, Inc.
For information about special discounts for bulk purchases, please contact Simon & Schuster Special Sales
at 1-866-506-1949 or business@simonandschuster.com.
The Simon & Schuster Speakers Bureau can bring authors to your live event. For more information or to book an event,
contact the Simon & Schuster Speakers Bureau at 1-866-248-3049 or visit our website at www.simonspeakers.com.
The text for this book was set in Acta Book.
The illustrations for this book were rendered in colored pencils on Arches watercolor paper.
Manufactured in China
0523 SCP
First Edition
2 4 6 8 10 9 7 5 3 1
Library of Congress Cataloging-in-Publication Data
Names: Bates, Amy June, author, illustrator.
Title: The welcome home / Amy June Bates.
Description: First edition. | New York : A Paula Wiseman Book, Simon & Schuster Books for Young Readers, [2023] |
Audience: Ages 4-8. | Audience: Grades K-1. | Summary: When Mr. and Mrs. Gargelson-Bittle decide life is too quiet,
they go in search of the perfect pet, but after welcoming a menagerie into their home, they still felt like something
is missing, until a puppy shows up at their doorstep, and now their family is complete.
Identifiers: LCCN 2022051365 (print) | LCCN 2022051366 (ebook) |
ISBN 9781534492325 (hardcover) | ISBN 9781534492332 (ebook)
Subjects: CYAC: Pets—Fiction. | Families—Fiction. | LCGFT: Picture books.
Classification: LCC PZ7.B2944446 We 2023 (print) | LCC PZ7.B2944446 (ebook) | DDC [E]—dc23
LC record available at https://lccn.loc.gov/2022051365
LC ebook record available at https://lccn.loc.gov/2022051366

The WELCOME HOME

AMY JUNE BATES

A Paula Wiseman Book
Simon & Schuster Books for Young Readers
New York   London   Toronto   Sydney   New Delhi

Mr. and Ms. Gargleson-Bittle
were missing something.

They tried eating waffles,

but that only helped for a moment.

Mr. Gargleson wanted something soft to cheer him up.

Ms. Bittle wanted something waggy to cheer her up.

They both wanted something a little bit lick-your-face-play-fetch-roll-over-rub-its-belly-and-chase-its-tail.

So they decided to get . . .

a snail.

The snail was soft.
"How nice," they cooed.
The snail was slow, and a little slimy, they admired
as they watched it make its way across the table.

They loved their little snail friend and named him Gordon.
But they thought they might also like something more . . .
something more waggy, perhaps?

So they decided to get . . .

an elephant.

They named her Louise.

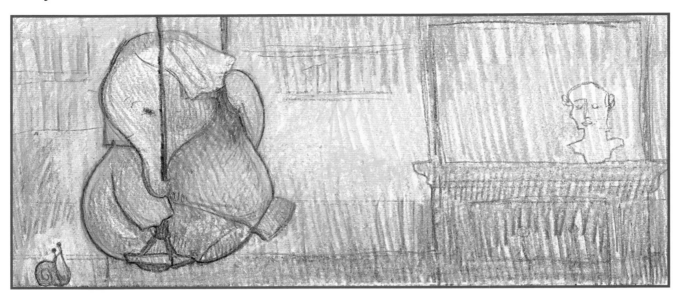

Louise's trunk definitely wagged back and forth.

"How splendid," they said as they watched
Gordon and Louise awkwardly play together.

They loved Louise and Gordon, but they thought their home might also need something a little less or perhaps something a little more . . . lick-your-face, perhaps?

So they got . . .

an aardvark

named Sam

and a whale

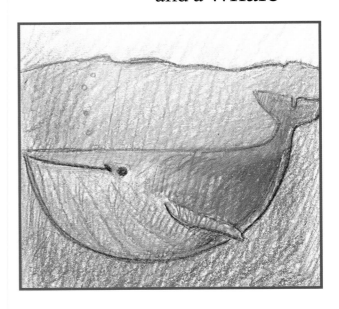

named Eugene.

The whale and the snail fell in love immediately.

Sam the aardvark was a bit of a loner, but he loved the Gargleson-Bittles and could lick their faces from all the way across the pool.

"Delightful," said Mr. and Ms. Gargleson-Bittle.

However, they did wonder, a little,
what it would be like to play fetch.

So they got a cat named Mork.

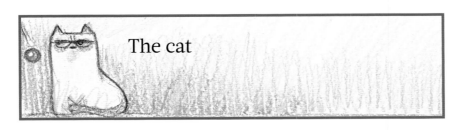 The cat

 did not

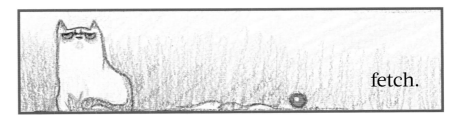 fetch.

Mork sat high up on Louise's back and was quite happy there.

Soon they got Wiggy and Tuna, two goldfish; Hortense, Hilda, and Javier, three hedgehogs; a giant panda named Peanut; twin seals, Freckles and Spectacles; an orangutan named Agnes; and a tiny armadillo named Cauliflower.

They all could roll over, but none of them would play fetch.

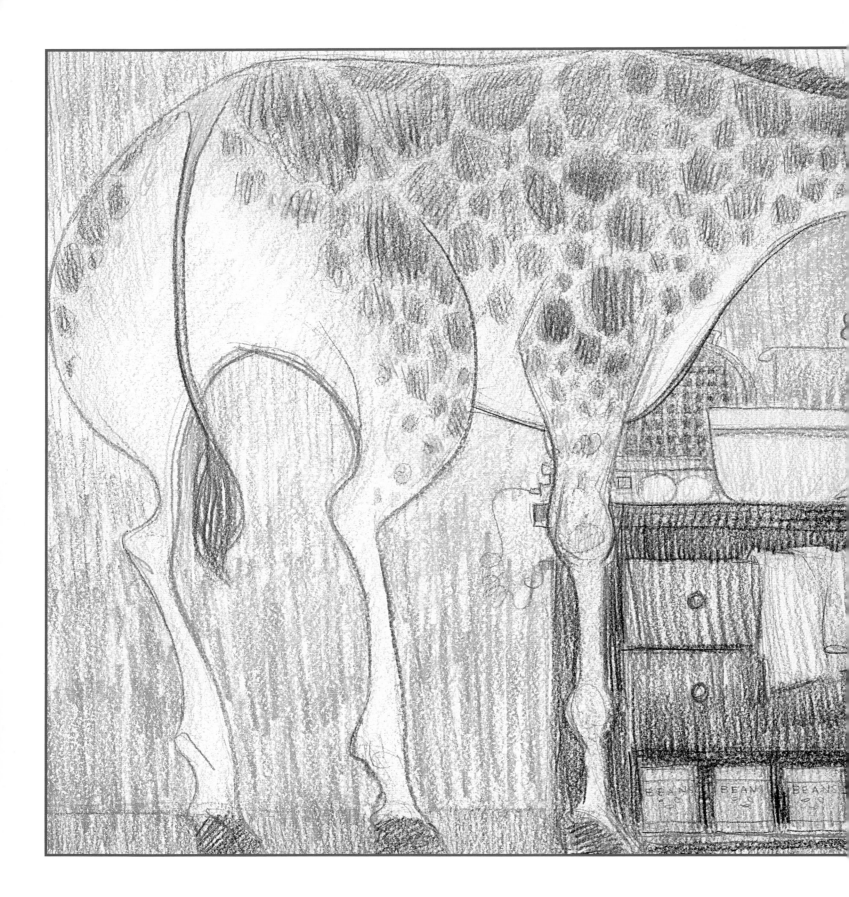

On the other hand, Oliver the octopus and Gerome the giraffe were quite good at fetch.

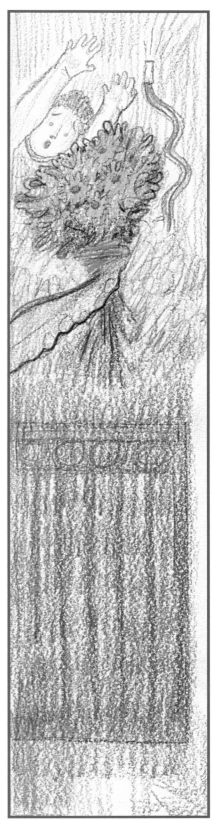

They could fetch cookies from the top shelf, canned beans from
the bottom shelf, and flowers from the neighbor's garden.

Bertie, a **buffalo**, and Willard, a **wombat**, loved belly rubs.
Paz the **snake** could chase his tail, and the **owls**—Zach, Zeke, Zora,
and Zeferino—could dig holes.
The **toads**—Robert, Ribbet, and Omar—could bark.
Acorn, Pigeon, and Cheese—the **raccoons**—loved going on long walks.

Everyone found out that Madame Pickles, the donkey, was
surprisingly good at howling at the moon.

"This is the life," said Mr. Gargleson.

"Luxury," said Ms. Bittle as a flock of ducklings hatched in
her hair. (Jill, Jam, Jumbo, Jaydon, Jake, Jump, Jeans, and Jupiter.)

The Gargleson-Bittles were happy.
Their house definitely wasn't too quiet.
And it definitely wasn't the same.

But they sometimes sighed very quietly, wondering
if there wasn't something still missing.
Just then they heard a little scratching at their door.

There on their doorstep was a very soft, very waggy, very lick-your-face-play-fetch-roll-over-rub-its-belly-and-chase-its-tail sort of a thing.

"I wonder what it is?" they said.

"It doesn't matter. We'll name him Waffles," they said.

The Gargleson-Bittles were now perfectly happy and quite content.